DREAMWORKS

SHE-RA
AND THE
PRINCESSES OF POWER

ORIGIN OF A HERO

BY TRACEY WEST
ILLUSTRATED BY AMANDA SCHANK

SCHOLASTIC INC.

ISBN 978-1-338-29841-3

10 9 8 7 6 5 4 3 2 1   19 20 21 22 23

Printed in the U.S.A. 23

First printing 2019

Book design by Carolyn Bull

CONTENTS

THE WORLD OF

ETHERIA

On a planet called Etheria, two forces battle for control.

The Horde, with its skillfully trained soldiers and advanced technology, has one goal: to conquer all of Etheria in the name of Hordak.

The other force, the Rebellion, is made up of princesses from across the planet and has been fighting to maintain harmony and freedom for all of Etheria's inhabitants. But a series of heartbreaking defeats left their alliance broken, with the princesses looking out for their own kingdoms instead of working together.

Hidden among them all is a hero to be. Her destiny was written by the First Ones a thousand years ago. Now she is about to rise again, and the future of Etheria lies in her hands.

As her story unfolds, meet her and some of the characters who will help determine her fate . . .

ADORA

Raised by the Horde, Adora believed she was doing good. But when she finds a mythical sword that unlocks her power as She-Ra, Adora is driven to fight for Etheria as a leader of the Rebellion.

ABILITIES: Adora is a clever problem solver, a fast and athletic soldier, and a brave fighter.

SHE-RA

When Adora raises her sword and pledges to fight "for the honor of Grayskull," she is transformed into the mythical warrior princess She-Ra. Adora retains her personality and sense of self, but she's taller and stronger—and has much better hair.

POWERS: Super-strength, shape-shifting sword, limited healing powers, connection to the ancient First Ones of Etheria

THE HORDE

CATRA

Catra and Adora were both orphans and were close growing up in the Horde; they thought of themselves as sisters. Catra is a prankster with a villainous streak that she is forced to explore once Adora discovers the sword.

ABILITIES: She's cunning and fast, with catlike reflexes.

SHADOW WEAVER

This scheming sorceress was the closest thing Adora and Catra had to a mother when they were growing up. Her mask hides more than her face . . . it hides the secret to her mysterious past.

POWERS: Sorcery and control of shadows

HORDAK

The evil leader of the Horde is bent on world domination. The Horde recruits rarely see him, as he prefers to plot from the depths of his lab.

ABILITIES: He has a brilliant technological mind.

THE REBELLION

GLIMMER

The princess of Bright Moon is driven to find her own path and is an enthusiastic leader of the Rebellion. She has inherited magical powers from her mother, but her magic is limited, which can make her feel insecure at times.

POWERS: Teleportation, energy blasts, sparkle powers

BOW

Glimmer's best friend is a good guy who values loyalty and honor above everything else. He will do anything for his friends—and even complete strangers.

ABILITIES: He's an expert archer and a whiz with technology.

QUEEN ANGELLA

She is Glimmer's mother and the immortal queen of Bright Moon. After the tragic death of her husband at the hands of the Horde, she is overprotective of her daughter.

POWER: Flight

CHAPTER 1
ADORA AND CATRA

"Look, Catra! This one is shaped like a perfect circle!"

Adora scrambled across the pile of rubble toward Catra and dropped the shiny stone into her palm.

For best friends, the two girls looked as different as night and day: Adora, with her sandy-blonde hair in a neat ponytail and her slender build. Catra, with her feline ears sticking out of her wild mane of dark brown hair, and her striking eyes: one turquoise and one golden yellow.

Catra held the blue stone up to the light between two fingers, her nails as sharp as claws.

"Nice one!" she said.

"Keep it," Adora told her.

Catra grinned. "Nah—you can keep it. It matches your eyes."

"Aw, you are so sweet," Adora replied.

"Ew! You did *not* just say that about me. Take it back!" Catra protested.

Adora laughed and slipped the stone into a pocket on her utility belt—part of the standard uniform for Horde recruits.

Adora had been wearing a similar uniform since she could remember. Shadow Weaver told her she'd been abandoned in the Fright Zone as a baby and adopted by the Horde. That was all she knew about her past.

She didn't think about it much. There was little time for daydreaming when you were a Horde recruit. They trained from sunup until long after the sun went down. But there were a few pockets of free time here and there. Those she usually spent with Catra.

Adora got back to searching the rock pile for treasures. The two girls had discovered the rubble stash when they were little. Even though they were teenagers now, they still came back. The stones were bright spots of color in the Fright Zone, a sprawling compound of cold metal buildings and spiraling black towers, all bathed in a dank, smoky haze of pollution from the factories. Topping it all off was a constant low, mechanical hum that never stopped. The rock pile was a haven, a place all their own.

Of course, it was hard to keep anything secret from Shadow Weaver.

"What are you doing, wasting your time in that pile of trash?" she'd asked the girls.

"It's not trash!" Catra had argued.

Adora had backed her up. "The rocks are pretty!"

They'd proudly showed her the smooth stones shaped like clouds and beetles and sprockets. Shadow Weaver had laughed.

"They're nothing more than chunks of silica altered by the heat of the weapons foundry," she said.

But she hadn't stopped them from going there.

"Have you found anything?" Adora asked Catra.

Catra kicked the rubble. "Nothing."

The tech device on Adora's wrist let out a beep. "Hey, we've gotta run! Training starts in three minutes!"

Catra leapt off the rubble pile with feline grace. "Last one there has to mop the barracks!"

Adora jumped to her feet. Catra made everything a competition. "No fair! You've got a head start!"

She raced across the Horde compound, located in the heart of the Fright Zone. Catra was fast, but she was showing off, jumping across the metal rooftops of the soldiers' quarters. Adora simply ran as fast as she could, taking a direct path to the training center.

Breathless, she arrived at the door at the exact moment Catra jumped down from the roof.

"Tie!" Adora announced.

"Really?" Catra asked. "Because I'm pretty sure my foot touched the floor right before you got here."

Adora grabbed her by the arm and pulled her inside. "Come on! We don't want to be late."

The two girls ran into the training room and slid into their seats next to Lonnie, Kyle, and Rogelio, members of their cadet team. Strong and tough, Lonnie wore her hair in long braids. Rogelio, a green lizard humanoid, combined agility and raw power in training exercises. Then there was Kyle. The skinny boy with a mop of light brown hair was always trying to keep up with his teammates.

A buzzer blared, announcing the start of the session.

"All right, recruits," began Commander Cobalt, a tall, imposing leader covered in blue fur. "Today we are taking a break from learning about our evil princess overlords to review Beast Island."

"Isn't that where Catra's from?" joked Octavia. The tall girl with tentacle arms on her back led another team of recruits.

Catra growled and lunged forward. Adora pulled her back.

"Beast Island, again?" asked Lonnie. "We've been hearing about it since we were little."

"That's right," Commander Cobalt said. "We teach it every year so you don't forget. Break a rule and you will be sent to Beast Island. End of story."

"So, um, what kind of beasts are we talking about?" asked Kyle. "Nobody ever really says."

Rogelio grunted in agreement.

"Dangerous beasts," Commander Cobalt replied.

"Yeah, but how dangerous, exactly?" Kyle asked. "Like, incinerate-you-with-one-fiery-breath kind of dangerous? Or chase-you-around-until-you-get-tired kind of dangerous?"

"Stop asking so many questions, cadet!" Commander Cobalt barked. "That goes for every-one. You sit. You listen. You remember. No questions. Got it?"

"Yes, Commander," everyone responded. Catra looked at Adora and rolled her eyes. Adora giggled.

The commander glared at the girls. "I highly suggest if you want to get anywhere in the Horde, you take this training seriously."

Adora straightened up. "Yes, Commander!" she said crisply.

Commander Cobalt spent the rest of the session reciting a long list of things that could get you sent to Beast Island.

"Disobeying a direct order from Hordak. Entering secure zones without permission. Stealing ration bars . . ."

Adora took careful notes. She'd heard a rumor that Shadow Weaver was going to choose a new force captain soon. She wanted to make sure she was considered.

Keep your eyes on the prize, Adora, she told herself.

Finally, a buzzer sounded.

"Yeah!" cheered Kyle. "Lunchtime!"

The students filed out of the building. As usual, the recruits stuck with the members of their training teams. Adora, Catra, Lonnie, Kyle, and Rogelio stepped out into the afternoon heat together.

"Anyone know what kind of ration bars we get today?" Kyle asked. "I hope it's the beige ones."

"Beige? Are you crazy?" Adora said. "Everyone knows the gray ones are the best."

"I kind of like the brownish-greenish ones," Lonnie said.

"Ugh!" Catra cried. "Those taste like . . . like bugs!"

"Really? Have you ever eaten a bug?" Lonnie asked.

Catra grimaced. "Are you serious? No way!"

Lonnie turned to face Rogelio, walking backward. "I bet you've eaten a few bugs, Rogelio. What do you think? Are they tasty?"

Rogelio shrugged his scaly shoulders.

Adora smiled. She felt pretty lucky to be assigned to this team. Everybody had their strengths and weaknesses, but they all worked together pretty well. She was glad to call them not only teammates, but friends.

Pounding footsteps pulled Adora out of her thoughts.

"Lonnie!" Adora grabbed her and pulled her out of the way just in time. A squad of Horde soldiers marched past the group. They looked unstoppable in their head-to-toe gray armor. Helmets hid their faces, with a panel of glowing light where their eyes should have been.

"I heard they're liberating a place called Elberon today," Lonnie whispered. "It's an outpost of Bright Moon."

Adora shuddered at the words *Bright Moon*. The capital of Etheria was run by princesses— cruel rulers who wanted to bring darkness and destruction to their planet. The Horde had been bravely fighting to take control of the kingdom for years now.

"I wish I were going," Catra muttered. "See the world outside the Fright Zone for once."

"Me too," Adora agreed.

She watched the squad march off, led by their brave force captain.

That'll be me someday, Adora vowed to herself. *When I'm force captain, my team will kick some serious princess butt. We'll free Etheria from their harsh rule forever!*

CHAPTER 2
PRINCESS GLIMMER BREAKS THE RULES

Thud!

Princess Glimmer landed on the floor of the room she'd been staying in for the last couple of weeks. She had managed to successfully jump from the rocking chair to the side table. Then she'd leapt and grabbed the chandelier hanging from the ceiling. It had swung back and forth wildly, and she'd lost her grip.

She jumped to her feet as the door opened. A woman in a forest-green gown, with hair piled on top of her head and wings fluttering on her back, rushed in.

"Your Highness, are you all right?" the woman asked. "My attendant tells me you've refused to come to the harp recital. And then I heard that terrible crash!"

"I'm fine, Mayor," Glimmer said. She blew a stray strand of pink hair away from her face.

"If you're fine, then please join us for the recital," the mayor of Elberon urged.

"I can't. I'm training," Glimmer replied, jumping back onto the rocking chair. She struggled to keep her balance.

The mayor sighed. "I don't understand all this training, Princess. Elberon is the safest village in all of Etheria. We are far from Bright Moon and were never attacked even once during the great wars of the past."

Glimmer leapt toward the high dresser, grabbing the top with her hands and then pulling herself up. "My mother sent me to Elberon to protect you," she replied with a grunt. "And that's what I'm going to do."

"In that case," the mayor said, "I humbly request your presence at the harp recital, where everyone will be. If we were to be attacked, what good would you be to us here in your room?"

Glimmer jumped off the dresser and somersaulted across the rug. Then she hopped to her feet.

"Fine," Glimmer said. "But I am not going there to have fun. I will be there as a guard whose duty it is to keep the entire room safe!"

"As you wish, Princess," the mayor said. She left the room, sweeping her long skirt after her with a flourish.

Glimmer hurtled over an ottoman and followed the mayor outside. They joined a throng of winged villagers in brightly colored clothes, all of them headed for the celebration hall.

Glimmer shook her head as she watched their happy faces.

The people here act like nothing is wrong. Like the Horde isn't attacking all over Etheria more and more every day, destroying the peaceful, joyful planet we have worked so hard to build. These people go to their tea parties and harp recitals and pretend the Horde doesn't exist. It's a good thing Mom sent me here.

As soon as she had the thought, Glimmer realized something: Maybe that's exactly *why* Queen Angella had sent her to Elberon—because it was safe. Glimmer had begged and pleaded to have a bigger role in the resistance against the Horde. And instead of putting her on the front lines, her mother had sent her to the most boring village on all of Etheria.

Glimmer sighed and entered the hall. She positioned herself by the doorway while the others took their seats. As the harpist began playing a slow, joyless tune, Glimmer scanned the room for suspicious activity, but the only thing she caught was a small boy yawning.

His yawn was contagious. She leaned back against the wall, her eyes fluttering. The music was so mellow that after a while, she could hardly stay awake. Her eyes fluttered again . . .

"The Horde is coming!"

Glimmer snapped to attention. The harp music stopped. Everybody turned to see a breathless villager dressed in green. Glimmer could tell from his uniform that he was one of Elberon's sentries from the guard post at the edge of the woods.

The mayor stood up. "Arturo, what is this interruption?"

"We saw them!" he replied. "Making their way over the ridge, heading toward the forest. A platoon of soldiers, and a whole bunch of strange machines. It's the Horde, for sure!"

Glimmer ran forward. "We need to get the children to safety right away!" she cried. "Then everyone else needs to grab a weapon and—"

The mayor interrupted her. "Arturo, are you sure it's the Horde?"

"It's them," Arturo said. "But I'm afraid we can't fight them, Mayor. They outnumber us."

Panicked, the villagers began to all talk at once.

"I'll go with Arturo and join the sentries!" Glimmer shouted to the mayor. "We'll need to stop them before they make it past the woods."

The mayor shook her head. "You heard Arturo," she replied. "We must retreat."

Glimmer's purple eyes flashed. "Retreat? You're just going to let the Horde take over?"

"We have no choice," the mayor said.

"Of course we do!" Glimmer cried. "We can fight!"

Heart pounding, Glimmer grabbed Arturo by the arm and pulled him outside toward his horse.

"Princess, come back here!" the mayor yelled. "That's an order!"

Glimmer ignored her. She and Arturo climbed up and took the reins.

"Hurry!" Glimmer cried. "We don't have much time!"

Arturo hesitated.

"I'm a princess, Arturo," Glimmer said. "I out-rank the mayor. Let's go!"

Arturo nodded and spurred the horse on. They rode until they reached the forest. He stopped the horse at the outpost—four tall sentry towers that rose above the treetops.

They jumped off the horse and raced to the top of a sentry tower. Glimmer shouted out questions as they climbed.

"What kind of weapons do you have here?"

"Bows and arrows, mostly," Arturo replied. "The four of us are pretty good shots."

"Four," Glimmer repeated. She silently cursed herself for not checking this outpost before. If the only thing that stood between Elberon and the Horde were a few arrows, the village was in big trouble.

Instinctively, she extended her arms. Glowing sparkles jumped from her fingertips. She'd practiced using her sparkle powers before, but never in a real battle.

There's a first time for everything, Glimmer thought just as they emerged at the top of the tower and caught a glimpse of the approaching Horde.

Six gigantic, spiderlike robots led about two dozen troops. They weren't a huge army, but with their robots, armor, and laser weapons, they might as well have been two hundred.

Glimmer looked at the other towers. The three sentries had their bows loaded and arrows pointed at the incoming threat.

"Aim for any weak spots you see," Glimmer said to Arturo. "I'll try to jam their circuits."

"How will you do that?" Arturo asked, getting into position.

Glimmer grinned. "It's a princess thing."

"They're advancing!" one of the sentries called out.

The Horde robots scrambled down the hill on their metal legs. They stopped and scanned the forest edge with laser eyes. Then they aimed their cannons at the sentry towers.

A barrage of arrows shot down as the cannons' lasers flew up. Some arrows harmlessly bounced off the robots. One lodged in a port behind one of the spider-robots' heads, sending sparks flying.

"Hit the ports!" Glimmer yelled. "And watch out for me. I've got to get closer."

"Princess—" Arturo began.

Glitter closed her eyes and concentrated.

Pop!

She teleported from the top of the tower

down to the hill. Her whole body tingled with energy as she landed. It was the first time she'd teleported since she'd left Bright Moon. Her home kingdom was the source of her powers, so she didn't want to waste them in Elberon unless she really needed them.

Like now.

As Glimmer found her bearings, a robot leaned over her.

Zap! She hit it with a blast of sparkles. The robot froze, then began to sizzle.

"Yes!" Glimmer cheered.

"Glimmer, watch out!" Arturo called from the tower.

Glimmer spun around just as a robot fired a laser blast from one of its cannons.

Pop! She quickly teleported a few feet away. Then she zapped the robot with a sparkle blast, stopping it in its tracks.

Suddenly, a loud cry filled the air, and the Horde troops stormed down the hill.

"So you're not gonna let your robots do your

dirty work for you, huh?" Glimmer called out. The soldiers all trained their blasters on her.

Pop! Glimmer teleported behind enemy lines.

Zap! Zap! Zap! One by one, the confused soldiers fell to the ground, hit by her shimmering blasts.

Between Glimmer's sparkle powers and the well-aimed arrows of the sentries, the hill had become a heap of sparking, smoking metal and fallen troops.

"We did it!" Glimmer cried.

Then she heard a thundering noise behind her.

Another wave of robots and soldiers crested the top of the hill—twice as many as before.

"Uh-oh," Glimmer said. She balled her hands into fists and flung them out to hurl another sparkle blast. But only a few weak sparkles came out. Glimmer frowned. "Double uh-oh."

A robot had already trained its cannons on her. She closed her eyes and concentrated all her energy on teleporting.

Pop! She appeared back in the forest, behind the sentry towers. She needed time to think—and plan.

Suddenly, she felt herself being pulled onto a horse. The rider flung Glimmer up behind him.

"Hey!" she yelled.

The mayor rode up on a horse beside them. "We must retreat, Princess."

"No!" Glimmer cried. "We can't give up now! The arrows are working, and we—"

"We cannot win!" the mayor said. "But I can succeed in one thing—in my promise to your mother. I will get you back to her safely."

She nodded to the rider seated in front of Glimmer. "Take her to Bright Moon."

"No!" Glimmer objected.

The rider spurred on the horse. Glimmer watched, helpless, as one of the sentry towers crashed to the forest floor.

I may not have stopped the Horde this time, she thought. *But next time, I will.*

CHAPTER 3
SNAKE!

"Lights out!"

A buzzer sounded in the barracks of the Horde cadets, and the lights shut off. Streams of moonlight shone through the one tiny window on the metal wall, basking the room in a yellow glow.

Adora lay in bed, turning over the perfectly round stone in her hands. Catra dangled down from the top bunk.

"Whatcha doing?" Catra asked. Then she gracefully slid into Adora's bunk and sat cross-legged, watching her friend.

"Just thinking," Adora replied. "Have you ever felt a connection to something and you don't exactly know why?"

Catra frowned thoughtfully. "What do you mean?"

"Well, sometimes I feel like I want to know our world better. All the people in it, but also the planet itself." Adora held up the stone to Catra, imagining it was Etheria. "Like how we got here and stuff." She shook her head. It sounded weird now that she'd said it out loud.

"I know how we got here," Catra replied. "Nobody wanted us, so they dumped us here."

"That's not what I meant," Adora said. She sighed. "I can't wait until we go on missions. We'll finally see what's outside this place. We'll go to places we've never been and take them back in the name of Hordak."

"Yeah, that'll be amazing," Catra said. "Because the Fright Zone is totally boring. I almost fell asleep in Cobalt's class today."

"That's because class *was* boring," Adora said. "Except for Octavia being a jerk. Her whole team is so negative. If they were more confident in themselves, they wouldn't need to trash-talk everyone else."

Catra grinned. "Don't worry. Those guys won't be bugging us for a while."

Adora sat up. "What do you mean?"

"Aaaaaaieeeeeeeeeeeeeeeee!"

A loud scream rang through the barracks.

Catra's grin got wider. "Octavia must have found the little surprise I left for her."

"Catra . . ." Adora said, raising an eyebrow at her. "What did you do?"

Adora flipped on the lights and ran to Octavia's bunk. The other cadets were awake, thanks to Octavia's scream.

Octavia had jumped out of her bunk and was pointing to the bed.

"Snake!" she yelled.

Adora spotted a skinny black snake curled up on Octavia's pillow. She and Catra had often seen black snakes in the weeds next to the armory, and she knew they were harmless. But Octavia's

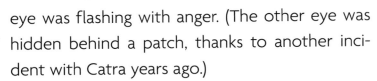

eye was flashing with anger. (The other eye was hidden behind a patch, thanks to another incident with Catra years ago.)

"It won't hurt you," Adora said to Octavia. "I'll get rid of it for you."

She reached past her to grab the snake, but Octavia pushed her.

"Your little friend is responsible for this!" she yelled. "And she's going to pay!" She sprinted toward Catra.

"Get her, Octavia!" someone yelled, and soon the loud cheers of the recruits filled the barracks.

Not again, Catra, Adora thought. *Can't you stay out of trouble for just one day?*

Adora picked up the snake and dropped it out the nearest window. Then she ran back to her bunk to find Catra and Octavia in a wrestling match on the floor. A circle of recruits surrounded them.

"Scratch her other eye out, Catra!" yelled one girl.

"Show her who's boss, Octavia!" shouted one of Octavia's teammates.

Catra yanked on Octavia's hair.

"Ow!" Octavia shrieked. She grabbed Catra by the ankles and lifted her above her head.

"Body slam! Body slam! Body slam!" the cadets began to chant.

Catra tried to kick out of the hold and almost succeeded, but Octavia's teammate joined the fight and pinned Catra's arms behind her back.

Adora glanced over at Lonnie, Rogelio, and Kyle. They were cheering on the fight, but nobody was moving to help Catra. Adora couldn't stand by and let Octavia win an unfair fight, even if Catra had started it.

"Yaaaaaaa!" With a cry, Adora jumped up and pulled the guy off Catra. Then she delivered a double kick to the back of Octavia's knees. Octavia buckled and loosened her grip on Catra, who tumbled to the floor.

Adora grabbed Octavia from behind and wrestled her to the ground.

"Get off me!" Octavia shrieked.

"Hold her down, Adora!"

Adora's head snapped toward the sound of Catra's voice. Her friend was crouched on the top bunk, ready to spring.

Catra leapt. She landed on Octavia and pinned her down by the shoulders. One of the recruits dropped to her knees and tapped the floor with her hand.

"One . . . two . . . three!" the girl cried. "Catra wins!"

Cheers and boos erupted in the barracks. Catra jumped up and pumped her fist in the air. Adora let go of Octavia's arms.

"I got rid of the snake," she told her.

Octavia snarled and stomped away. The other recruits returned to their bunks.

Catra grinned at Adora.

"That was fun," she said.

Adora shook her head. "If Shadow Weaver's going to choose a new force captain soon, we need to stay out of trouble. It's a good thing she didn't—"

"Didn't what?" Shadow Weaver's voice cut in.

Adora froze at the sound.

CHAPTER 4
COMMANDER'S PET

Great, Catra said to herself. *Doesn't Shadow Weaver ever sleep?*

"I find it difficult to believe that you cadets are making noise when there is a training exercise tomorrow," Shadow Weaver said in her deep, spooky voice. The commander floated a few inches off the ground in the doorway of the barracks. As always, her black hair swirled above her head, a dark mask hid her face, and flowing, deep red robes covered her body.

"We were training for the exercise," Catra lied.

"If only I believed you, Catra," Shadow Weaver said. "Adora, couldn't you have stopped your fellow cadets from this nonsense?"

Catra rolled her eyes. *Here it comes.*

"Everyone is just excited about the exercise tomorrow," Adora said.

Catra shook her head. One thing you could always count on was Adora sucking up to Shadow Weaver.

"That's enough excitement," Shadow Weaver said. "If I hear another noise tonight, there will be consequences!"

Shadow Weaver swept out of the barracks, and the girls quickly climbed into their bunks. Catra slid under the covers and let herself purr at the memory of tonight's events. She was just about asleep when Adora's head popped up next to her pillow.

"Did you have to do that to Octavia?" Adora whispered. "You almost got us into trouble."

Catra stopped purring. "Relax. Shadow Weaver's bark is worse than her bite. Besides, it was worth it, wasn't it?" She propped herself up on an elbow. "I will *never* forget Octavia's scream."

Adora giggled. "That *was* pretty funny." She did a couple pull-ups on the edge of the bunk.

"But now I'm all hyped up. I need sleep so I can do my best tomorrow, but how am I supposed to sleep after that?"

Catra ran one claw along the edge of the bunk near Adora's face. "Oh, come on. You'll hardly have to try tomorrow. Shadow Weaver thinks everything you do is great."

"That's not true!" Adora protested, but they both knew it was. Once, both girls had climbed to the roof of the weapons foundry, and Shadow Weaver had caught them. She'd scolded Catra for breaking the rules and praised Adora for her climbing skills.

"Whatever," Catra said. She grinned. "You may not need to rest for training, but you *do* need some beauty sleep!"

"Very funny," Adora replied. She tossed a pillow at Catra before ducking back down to her own bunk.

Catra settled into her bed and stared at the ceiling. Now *she* couldn't sleep.

The relationship between Catra, Adora, and

Shadow Weaver had always been a complicated one.

Catra couldn't remember anything from before she arrived in the Fright Zone, a tiny girl in a big place filled with people and noise and machines. The first friendly face she had seen was Adora's, a face her own height, with big blue eyes.

Catra learned that Adora had come to the Fright Zone as a baby, and Shadow Weaver had taken Adora under her wing. And when Adora had latched on to Catra, Shadow Weaver became Catra's mentor, too.

Maybe if I'd been here before Adora, I'd be Shadow Weaver's favorite, Catra mused, not for the first time.

She rolled onto her side and grabbed the end of her tail—something she did whenever she couldn't sleep. A spot near the end was always tender, left over from that time their cadet team had dared each other to see who could get closest to the incinerator. After Catra burned her tail, the others had scattered. But Adora held Catra's hand all the way back to the barracks, and then snuck into the infirmary to get supplies to treat the burn.

Adora sucks up to Shadow Weaver, Catra thought. *But she's been nice to me when nobody else was. What would I do without her?*

Catra drifted off to sleep, listening to Adora's breaths beneath her.

CHAPTER 5
EVALUATION DAY

Beep! Beep! Beep!

Adora had set her alarm to go off before dawn. She sprang out of bed, excited for the training exercise ahead.

I'll prove to everyone that I'm serious about this, she thought as she brushed her teeth in the cadets' locker room.

She spun around, delivering a roundhouse kick to a punching bag hanging from a metal beam on the ceiling. Then she spun back to the sink, spat out a mouthful of gray toothpaste, and rinsed with the always-ice-cold water that came out of the tap.

She quickly suited up into her Horde uniform and slicked her hair back into a ponytail.

As she jogged out of the room, she passed another punching bag, this one with an image of a princess on the side.

"Hey, Princess! You lookin' at me?" Adora asked it.

She spun around again, delivering a roundhouse kick to the princess. Her foot smacked into it with a satisfying sound.

Punching bags are fun, Adora thought, *but real princesses will be even better!*

A red light flashed on the wall as a siren blared throughout the barracks. Then a voice rang out over the speakers.

"All squadrons, report to the training area immediately for evaluation."

Adora darted out of the locker room. She raced through the hallways to the training course, where she quickly slipped into her gear: arm and leg guards, a glowing breastplate, a weapons belt with an extendable staff, and special training goggles that allowed the cadets to see the holograms in the training arena.

Lonnie and Rogelio arrived next, followed by

Kyle, who was puffing and panting with the effort of getting there on time. They slipped into their armor, too.

"Anyone seen Catra?" Adora asked.

The rest of her teammates just shrugged.

"Not *again*," Adora groaned.

Catra doesn't take anything seriously! We'll never get assigned to a squad if she keeps this up!

Adora and her teammates stepped up to two metal doors at the entrance of the training arena. A Horde sergeant approached.

"At attention, cadets!" he barked, pacing back and forth in front of them. "Your simulation is about to begin. Here's your scenario. You'll be passing through the treacherous Whispering Woods to reach the heart of the rebel insurgency, Bright Moon."

Next to Adora, Kyle gulped. Every recruit knew that the Whispering Woods was one of the most dangerous places on the planet. But Adora wasn't afraid.

"Your mission is to defeat the queen of the princesses and liberate Bright Moon in Lord

Hordak's name," he continued. Then he stopped. "Where is Catra?"

"She will be here. I promise," Adora said.

The sergeant scowled and made a note on his data pad. "Mm-hmm," he said. Then he raised his voice again. "The Whispering Woods is full of princesses—vicious, violent instigators. They will take you out if given the chance. Don't give in to them. Good luck, recruits."

Adora's heart raced as the metal doors slid open. She stepped into the training arena, followed by Lonnie, Kyle, and Rogelio.

They cautiously walked into a forest of metal columns standing in for trees. Adora tensed as a rumbling sound filled the room. A troop of round-bodied robots rolled through the trees, projecting princess holograms. To the cadets, it looked like the princesses were shooting laser blasts from stun guns on their chests.

"Watch out!" Adora cried.

She dodged a laser. Kyle gave a frightened yelp but managed to get out of the way, too.

Zap! Zap! Zap! The princesses shot their lasers.

Adora and her team expertly shielded themselves as they made their way deeper into the forest.

Then . . .

"Ahhhhhhhhh!"

Kyle let out a scream as a stun bolt hit him dead-on. He fell to the ground, his body crackling with energy. His glowing chest plate flickered out, replaced by a red X.

"Aw, dang it," Kyle said.

"Seriously, Kyle?" Adora asked.

Kyle's eyes got wide as he looked past them. Adora, Lonnie, and Rogelio spun around to see four robot-princesses behind them.

"Run!" Adora yelled.

The three remaining team members took off, racing past the forest of columns and through a metal door. On the other side, they found a floor covered in a pattern of large tiles. The doors closed, trapping the robots behind them.

Adora and her teammates scanned the room, searching for some sign of their next challenge.

"Adora!" Lonnie yelled.

Adora leapt aside just as the tile beneath her feet flashed red and then dropped away, leaving a hole. More tiles followed and the hole got bigger.

Before Adora could think what to do next, an enormous robot floated up from the pit. It landed on the arena floor with four metal, spiderlike legs. The center of its body was a silver ball topped with laser cannons. It projected a giant hologram of a pink princess with an evil grin.

Boom! Laser bolts shot from her fingertips, and the team scattered. Where the lasers hit, the tiles dropped away.

This must be the queen, Adora thought. *Well, bring it on, Your Majesty!*

She grabbed the extendable staff from her belt and used it to launch herself up toward the robot. She hit one of its glowing eyes, then thrust the stick into its metal head. The robot exploded, sending Adora flying as it toppled partway back into the pit.

Adora landed, facedown, on a small area of remaining tiles. Two clawed feet walked past her. Catra had shown up after all.

Catra kicked the robot the rest of the way into the pit. Then she smirked at Adora and pointed to the tile Adora was lying on. It flashed red. Then it dropped.

Thinking quickly, Adora swung her staff across the top of the hole. It caught and she dangled above the abyss as Catra peered over the edge.

"Hey, Adora. How's it hanging?"

"Catra!" Adora said. "Did you really show up late and let us do all the hard parts? That is low, even for you."

"Aw, you know nothing's too low for me," Catra replied.

"Training exercise successfully completed," came a voice over the speakers.

Catra reached down and offered Adora a hand. "Come on, you look stupid hanging down there."

CHAPTER 6
A BITTERSWEET REWARD

By the time Adora and Catra reached the locker room, Adora had stopped being annoyed with her friend. It was a team exercise, after all, and they had succeeded as a team.

"You should have seen your face," Catra teased as they took off their training gear. "You were like, 'Aahh! Noooo! Betrayal!'"

"Oh come on, Catra, we're senior cadets now," Adora replied. "I can't believe you're still pulling such childish, immature—" She stopped and pointed behind Catra. "Is that a mouse?"

Catra whirled around, panicked. "What? Where?"

Adora laughed. "Are you ever going to *not* fall for that?"

Catra got defensive. "I dunno, are you ever going to let it go? That was *one* time."

"I know, but for some reason it's always funny!" Adora shot back.

We're not exactly even, Adora thought, *but it's something.*

"Adora!"

Shadow Weaver's voice made them both freeze. Adora snapped to attention and saluted.

"Shadow Weaver."

"You have done well," Shadow Weaver said, her hair floating behind her. "You have completed your training course in record time."

"Uh, well, that wasn't just me you know," Adora replied. "Catra did, too."

Shadow Weaver's gaze turned to Catra. "Ah, yes. How someone as unmotivated as you completed the course in time, I'll never know."

"Always serving up those pep talks, huh, Shadow Weaver?" Catra mumbled.

"Silence," Shadow Weaver said sternly. "Do not be flippant with me, cadet."

The room went dark, and shadowy tendrils snaked toward Catra. Adora tensed. The commander's shadow powers still freaked her out sometimes.

Catra's shoulders slumped. "Sorry, Shadow Weaver."

The tendrils receded. "Adora, walk with me," Shadow Weaver said.

Adora cast an apologetic look at Catra, who groaned and rolled her eyes.

It's not my fault Shadow Weaver gives Catra a hard time, Adora thought as she followed the commander. *Shadow Weaver's tough on everybody. And maybe if Catra would play by the rules once in a while . . .*

"Lord Hordak has been watching you," Shadow Weaver said as they moved together down the hall. "He thinks you are a fine candidate for force captain."

Adora stopped walking. "*Force captain?* Lord Hordak said that about *me*?"

Adora was used to praise from Shadow Weaver. But she wasn't expecting praise from Hordak.

"Oh yes," Shadow Weaver replied as they began walking again. "He sees great promise in you. In fact, he has given you the honor of leading a squadron in the invasion of the rebel fortress of Thaymor."

"Thaymor?" Adora asked in thrilled disbelief. "You mean we're finally seeing active duty?"

"*You* are seeing active duty," Shadow Weaver corrected.

Adora frowned. "But I'll be able to bring my team along, right?"

Shadow Weaver shook her head. "Your team is not ready. They'll only slow you down."

Adora took a deep breath. "Shadow Weaver, with respect, they've been training hard for this, too," she said. "And Catra—all she wants is to get out there and prove herself."

"Then she should have worked harder to prove herself to *me*." She pressed a shiny force captain badge bearing the Horde logo into Adora's hand.

"This is what I've raised you for, Adora," she said. "Now is your chance to prove yourself."

Adora stared at the badge, her eyes wide with awe.

Shadow Weaver stopped in front of a window with a view of the Fright Zone, a sprawling mass of steel-and-concrete buildings. She put an arm around Adora's shoulder.

"I saw talent in you from the moment I found you as an orphan child and took you in," she said. "Is this not what you have wanted since you were old enough to want anything?"

"Yes," Adora replied.

It is what I've always wanted . . . but not like this, she thought. Maybe I could ask Shadow Weaver to give my team another chance . . .

"With you at the forefront, we will crush the Bright Moon Rebellion once and for all," Shadow Weaver said. "Do not disappoint me."

Then she turned with a swirl of her cloak and vanished.

CHAPTER 7
BACK IN BRIGHT MOON

Despite Glimmer's protests, the horseman would not change course. After hours of riding, Glimmer accepted her fate. When they finally reached Bright Moon, she was exhausted and resentful.

Castle guards escorted her directly to her mother's throne room. Queen Angella looked as beautiful as always, with her long, flowing hair and gossamer wings. But her face was cold as she stared at Glimmer.

Glimmer knelt before Angella.

"Your Majesty," Glimmer said, because even though Angella was her mother, she was still her queen. Then Glimmer stood.

"I'm told you disobeyed orders and led the Rebellion into a dangerous combat situation after you were ordered to retreat," Queen Angella said.

"I was trying to protect a village from falling into the Horde's grasp!" Glimmer protested.

"You were reckless and put yourself and the other rebels in danger," Angella scolded.

"Fighting is SUPPOSED to be dangerous," Glimmer shot back. "How are we going to hold our own against the Horde if we keep retreating? Pretty soon we won't have anything left to defend!"

"I'm growing tired of your back talk, Commander Glimmer," Angella said.

"Why did you even make me a commander if you won't let me fight?" Glimmer asked.

Angella's dark eyes flashed. "That's enough. You're grounded!"

Glimmer groaned. "Ugh. Mom!"

"You heard me."

"You never let me do anything!" Glimmer complained.

"We are not having this discussion tonight," Angella said calmly. "You are embarrassing me in front of my royal court."

Glimmer put her hands on her hips. "Oh, *I'm* embarrassing *you*?"

"Go to your room!" Angella said firmly.

"I'm going!" Glimmer shouted.

Then she stormed out of the throne room.

How can I ever be a Rebellion commander if Mom won't let me rebel against anything?!

CHAPTER 8

INTO THE WHISPERING WOODS

Catra watched Adora leave with Shadow Weaver. When they were out of sight, she kicked a chair.

What does Shadow Weaver know? Catra wondered. *I'm the one who finished off that robot, anyway. Not Adora.*

She did her best to shake off the mood. The training exercise was over, and that meant there was at least an hour before lunch. She and Adora had been wanting to climb up to the water tower again. It had the best view of the Whispering Woods in the whole Fright Zone.

She dashed out of the locker room to search for Adora. Ten minutes later, she spotted her standing on one of the metal catwalks outside the building.

Catra pounced on Adora, knocking her to the ground.

"What'd Shadow Weaver say?" Catra asked. Then she spotted something shining in Adora's hand. "Hey, what's this?"

She took the object out of Adora's hand and climbed up to a support beam overhead, out of Adora's reach. She recognized the object immediately.

"No way! You've been promoted?" she asked.

"Well, kind of . . ." Adora said, avoiding Catra's eyes. "I mean, yeah, I guess. But it's not a big deal."

Catra's mind raced with possibilities. If Adora was a force captain, that meant their team would be at the front of the action. They'd be sent on important missions. She'd finally get to explore the world outside the Fright Zone! "Are you kidding? That is awesome!" Catra cheered. "We're gonna see the world—and conquer it! Adora, I *need* to blow something up!"

Adora looked away. "Um . . ."

Catra eyed her suspiciously. "What?"

"Shadow Weaver says you're not coming," Adora admitted.

Catra's pointy ears drooped. She knew Adora was Shadow Weaver's favorite, but she never imagined Shadow Weaver would separate them like this.

"What is her problem with me?!" Catra asked.

Adora faced her friend. "I mean . . . you *are* kind of disrespectful."

"Why should I respect her?" Catra fumed. "She's just bitter that she doesn't have any real power that doesn't come from Hordak, and everyone knows it." The next words came out of her mouth without thinking. "But I guess it sure must be easy being a people-pleaser like you."

Catra leapt from the beam to a higher platform.

"I am not a—" Adora began, but Catra wasn't in the mood to hear Adora defend herself. She jumped from the platform up to another catwalk and ran out of Adora's sight.

She climbed up higher and higher until she got to the very top of the building. It was her favorite place to come whenever she was upset—which was a lot—and nobody ever bothered her here, because nobody could climb so high. Nobody except Adora, anyway. Today, Catra hoped Adora hadn't followed her.

What's the point of training if I'm never going to get to go anywhere or do anything? she asked herself. She flipped Adora's badge over in her hands and stared out at the Fright Zone, lost in thought for who knows how long.

Around the time it started getting dark, she heard a clink of metal.

Adora's grappling hook looped around a pipe and she pulled herself up. Catra turned away from her.

"Look, I'm sorry," Adora said, sitting next to Catra. "I didn't even think you wanted to be a force captain."

"I don't," Catra protested. "Here, take your stupid badge." She flung it at Adora.

"Come on, Catra. This is what I've been working for my entire life," Adora said. "I was hoping you could be . . . I don't know . . . happy for me."

Catra leapt to her feet. She didn't really want to be mad at her friend. "Ugh, whatever. It's not like I even care. I just want to get out of this dump at some point before I die of boredom."

Adora smirked. "So let's go."

She held out a key dangling from a metal ring. Catra was confused. *That looked like a skiff key . . . had Adora snuck into the vehicle bay?*

"No way," Catra said.

"Way," Adora replied. "Come on!"

The two girls climbed down from the roof and made their way to a flat-bottomed skiff vehicle hidden behind a building.

"I take it all back," Catra said. "You're officially awesome. I can't believe you actually stole a skiff!"

"Borrowed," Adora corrected her. "Please don't make me regret this!"

Adora jumped in the driver's seat, and Catra climbed in behind her. Adora started the engine and the skiff hovered above the ground. They quietly soared away from the buildings and into the desert surrounding the Fright Zone.

But *ugh*. Adora was driving so *slowly*.

"I've always wanted to drive one of these things," Catra said, reaching across Adora to grab the rudder. She yanked it back, and the skiff rocketed ahead.

"Whoa!" Adora yelled. "Save us enough fuel to get back!"

"That is a problem for future Adora and Catra," Catra said with a grin.

Their hair whipped behind them as they zipped across the desert. The taste of freedom energized Catra, and she spurred the skiff on even faster.

Suddenly, Adora's voice called out in true panic.

"Whoa! Whoa! Catra!"

Catra looked up from the rudder to see a forest of dense trees ahead of them. She slammed on the brakes just in time, and the skiff skidded to a stop before it reached the tree line. The two girls stared at the dark, eerie forest. They heard a rustling chorus of whispers coming from inside.

"What's that noise?" Catra asked.

"I think this must be the Whispering Woods," Adora replied. "They say there are monsters in there and the trees move when you're not looking. Every Horde squadron they've sent in there has never come out again."

Well, we can change that, Catra thought. "Let's go in." She stomped on the accelerator and the skiff took off into the woods.

"Ahhhhhhhh!" shrieked Adora.

"Wooooooo-hooooo!" Catra cheered.

The skiff rocketed through the dense greenery, snapping vines and breaking branches as it carved a jagged path through the woods.

"Catra, slow down!" Adora begged.

Catra ignored her. This was the most fun she'd had in her whole life!

"Catra! Tree! TREE!" Adora yelled.

This time, Catra looked up—to see a massive tree in their path. She tried to steer away from it, but the skiff was going too fast. Adora grabbed the rudder and pulled up hard. The skiff rocketed upward just before hitting the tree and spiraled crazily through the maze of the tree's coiled limbs.

Then . . . *whomp!* A branch hit Adora, and the force of the impact sent her flying off the skiff.

"Adooooraaaaaaaaa!" Catra cried, trying to control the skiff. But Adora didn't answer. Only haunting whispers came from the mass of twisted branches.

Her friend was gone.

CHAPTER 9
BOW'S PLAN

Glimmer sat at her desk in Bright Moon and wrote in her diary.

"Dear Mom, I know you'll never read this, but I have to write it somewhere," she said out loud. "I feel like you don't respect me."

Whoosh! An arrow whizzed past Glimmer's ear! It stuck with a thud into the wall beside her. A note unfurled from the arrow's shaft: LOOK OUTSIDE.

Glimmer rolled her eyes, yanked the arrow from the wall, and then marched over to the open bedroom window.

"Watch it!" she called down in a loud whisper. "You almost hit me!"

A figure below pushed back its hood to reveal

the friendly face of a teenage boy. He grinned up at Glimmer.

"Hey, Glimmer!" he shouted.

"*Shhhh!*" Glimmer warned. "Bow, what are you doing here?"

Normally, Glimmer would have been thrilled to see her best friend. She had missed him while she was stuck in Elberon. But the last thing she needed was to get in more trouble with her mom.

"Come down here!" Bow shouted.

"I can't! I'm grounded!" Glimmer hissed.

"What?" Bow yelled. "I can't hear you!"

Glimmer sighed with frustration. She teleported out of her room in a flash of pink sparkles and appeared behind Bow, shouting in his ear.

"I'm GROUNDED!" she told him.

Bow jumped. "Ah!"

Glimmer grabbed him and teleported both of them back to her room.

"Ugh! I'm so mad at my mom!" she complained.

Bow nodded as he began to fold and pick up the clothes that Glimmer had strewn around the floor.

"Is this about the siege on Elberon?" he asked.

"I was just trying to defend another one of our villages from falling into the Horde's clutches!" she replied. "She stationed me all the way out there because it's too remote to ever get attacked, but then it did, and it was my ONE CHANCE to prove that I can do this. But she acts like I can't do anything because I'm just a princess. Ugh!"

She teleported up to her high, floating platform bed.

"That doesn't make sense," Bow said. "Everyone here is a princess! I'm, like, the only one who's not a princess."

Glimmer collapsed dramatically on her bed. "Tell that to my mom!"

Bow held up a folded sweater. "Hey, where does this go?"

"Bottom drawer," Glimmer instructed.

Glimmer sometimes wondered how she and Bow had become friends. Bow could be compulsively neat, and Glimmer was sometimes careless and messy. Glimmer knew that she could spark to anger in a flash, while Bow usually kept his cool. But they bonded over their love of Bright Moon, and their desire to keep it safe from the Horde.

"Anyway, your mom might have a point," Bow said. "The only reason you got out of there is because of your teleportation powers, and let's face it, they don't always work that well."

Glimmer scowled. "Looking for support here, Bow!"

He climbed the floating steps to join her. "I'm just saying, if you want to prove yourself, it's going to take more than running recklessly into any old battle. Luckily, I've got just the thing."

He pulled out a small scanner pad. "Check this out. I detected a piece of First Ones tech in the Whispering Woods. A pretty powerful one, too, by the size of these readings."

Glimmer perked up. *First Ones* was the name given to the first inhabitants of Etheria. Nobody knew much about them, but the traces they'd left behind were mysterious and impressive: ruins of beautiful buildings, a language that nobody could decipher, and, most important advanced technology. If someone could unlock First Ones technology, Glimmer knew they could win the war for control of Etheria.

"If you find this First Ones tech and bring it back," Bow said, "your mom is bound to be impressed."

Glimmer knew she had to do something big to show her mother she could lead the Rebellion. Maybe this was it.

"I'm in!" she told Bow.

Then she transported them both outside in a flurry of pink sparkles.

CHAPTER 10
ADORA'S VISION

Groaning, Adora picked herself up from the forest floor. She had landed in a small clearing. She looked up, but she didn't see or hear the skiff.

"Ugh," she said, touching her head. "Catra?"

There was no answer. A glow on the other side of the clearing caught her eye.

Is that a . . . sword? she thought. *Weird place for someone to store a weapon.* She crept closer.

The sword didn't look like any weapon she'd ever seen in the Horde. This sword was beautiful, with a blue gem embedded in the golden hilt. The sword itself was forged from a silvery blue metal that gleamed softly in the dim light.

She reached out to touch the hilt . . .

Whoosh! A huge beam of pure white light shot out of the sword, knocking Adora backward. She gasped as images appeared in the bright light surrounding her. They came quickly and made no sense. Lights . . . swirling colors . . . the cry of a baby . . . and finally, a cloudy image of a majestic woman holding the sword, her hair and cape flowing behind her.

Then she heard a voice . . . a voice that she somehow knew did not belong to the woman with the sword.

Balance must be restored. Etheria must seek a hero. Adora . . .

"Adora!"

Adora's eyes snapped open. Catra was leaning over her with concern on her face.

"Catra? What happened?" Adora asked, slowly sitting up.

"You fell out of the skiff after you drove it into a tree," Catra replied.

"No, you drove it into a tree!" Adora protested.

"Up for debate," Catra said. She held out her hand. "Come on, let's go."

I must have gotten knocked out, Adora realized, *and had some crazy dream.*

But when she stood up, she saw that she was in the same clearing as her vision. *It couldn't have been a dream!*

"Wait, where is it?" she asked. "Where'd it go?"

"What?" Catra asked.

"There was a sword," Adora said. "It was right here. I tried to touch it, but it got really bright."

"Are you brain damaged?" Catra asked in alarm. "Don't be brain damaged! Oh, Shadow Weaver's gonna kill me!"

"I'm not brain damaged!" Adora insisted. "It was here. I saw it."

"Well, there's nothing here now," Catra said. "So come on, let's go!" They hopped onto the skiff and sped back to the Fright Zone.

The next day, Adora attended training sessions as usual, but flashes of the vision she had seen kept popping into her brain. That night, Adora stared at the bottom of Catra's bunk, unable to sleep as the strange images played on a loop in her mind.

You conked your head when you fell, she reasoned. *That's probably all it is.*

But she could still hear the whispers. They grew louder and louder.

Stop it! she told herself. She rolled onto her side and squeezed her eyes shut, willing the noises to stop. But the whispers became more urgent, and then one clear voice rose above them.

Adora . . . Adora . . . ADORA!

Adora bolted upright in bed, sweating and breathing hard.

I have to go back to those woods.

She quietly slipped out of bed and pulled on her uniform. Then she left the barracks.

"Hey, where are you going?"

Catra had followed her out and was now sleepily rubbing her eyes.

"Back to the woods," Adora told her. "There's something I need to figure out."

Catra's eyes widened. "What?"

Adora spotted a security robot at the end of

the hall and quickly pulled Catra behind a pillar. It passed by them without noticing.

"What is wrong with you?" Catra hissed. "You've been acting weird ever since we got back from the woods. Are you sure you're not brain damaged?"

"Look, Catra, I know I saw something out there!" Adora replied. "I just need to get another look. It feels . . . important, somehow."

Catra nodded. "Sounds good! Let's go!"

"No, I don't want you getting in trouble on my behalf," Adora said firmly. She glanced down the hallway and then broke away from Catra.

"Just cover for me, okay? I'll be back before anyone knows I'm gone," she said.

"Adora!" Catra called after her, but she didn't follow.

Adora made her way back to the Whispering Woods. She didn't have the skiff this time, so she pushed her way through the thick underbrush, trying to find the clearing. Leaves and twigs snagged her hair as she walked.

"What are you doing out here, Adora?" she muttered to herself. "Catra's right. This is crazy. There's no sword. You just got hit on the head a little too hard. You should just go back home and forget about all of this . . ."

Then she spotted a large gash cut into the side of a tree—could it have been made when the skiff crashed? She moved the leaves aside to see a bright light.

Excited, she followed the light into the clearing—the same clearing she had been in last night! There, still buried in the dirt, the beautiful sword gleamed brightly. She stared at it in awe.

Then two figures stepped into the clearing. One, a boy carrying a bow and arrow. The other, a girl wearing a purple outfit and a sparkly blue cape.

Is she . . . a princess? Adora froze, shocked.

"Horde soldier!" the girl yelled.

Adora bolted for the sword, but the princess reached it first and grabbed it. Then she vanished in a shower of sparkles and reappeared on the other side of the clearing, still holding the sword.

Adora charged at her, but the princess tossed the sword to the boy. He dropped his bow and arrows to catch it but panicked as Adora whirled to face him.

"Give me the sword!" Adora yelled.

Pop! The princess teleported again, landing on Adora's back and pulling her hair. Adora yanked the princess off her and then grabbed a bola—a cord with a metal ball on each end—from her belt and threw it at the boy's ankles. He tripped, falling forward, and the sword dropped from his hands.

"Stand down!" Adora cried. "I don't want to hurt you!"

"Since when do Horde soldiers not want to hurt anyone?" the princess asked.

She threw a sphere of light at Adora's feet. It exploded into sparkles, and Adora couldn't see anything for a few seconds. When she could see again, the princess was heading for the sword. Adora tackled her, and the two of them wrestled on the ground.

She's strong! Adora realized. *But of course she is . . . she's a princess. Now if I can just . . .*

In the struggle, she managed to get one hand on the sword.

Whoosh! An explosion of energy burst from the sword, knocking Adora on her back and sending the other two tumbling.

All Adora could see was intensely bright white light.

Then it faded to black.

CHAPTER 11
LIGHT HOPE'S CHALLENGE

Adora blinked. She was standing inside a room that seemed to be made of glimmering stones. Light reflected from every surface. She spun around and saw the hologram of a woman—the woman she remembered from her first vision. White eyes glowed on her purple face, and she wore a long, flowing purple gown.

"Hello, Adora," the hologram said.

"Who are you?" Adora asked. "What's going on?"

"My name is Light Hope. I have been waiting a long time for you. But I could not reach you until you forged your connection with the sword."

"You sent the sword?" Adora asked.

"The sword is meant for you," Light Hope replied.

A hologram of the sword appeared between Adora and Light Hope. Adora reached for it, but her hand passed right through it.

"Etheria has need of you, Adora," Light Hope said. "Will you answer its call? Will you fight for the honor of Grayskull?"

"What are you talking about?" Adora asked. "What is—What's Grayskull? You're not making any sense! I don't understand."

"You will," Light Hope promised.

The vision began to break apart around them. Light Hope faded away.

"Wait!" Adora cried.

Light Hope disappeared.

What just happened? Adora asked herself as the Whispering Woods came back into focus.

She discovered that her hands were bound in front of her and the princess and the boy were leading her through the forest. The princess was holding the sword.

"Hey, she's awake, Glimmer!" the boy said.

"What happened?" Adora asked. She didn't like being tied up, but she was desperate to know more about the vision.

"Quiet, Horde spy!" the princess named Glimmer snapped. "I ask the questions. How did you make it this far into the Whispering Woods?"

"I just . . . walked in," Adora replied. "And I'm not a spy!"

Glimmer snorted. "Sure, sure. You just so happened to find yourself in the Whispering Woods, just like you happened to try and steal the sword."

"It's not yours!" Adora protested. "I found it first!"

"The Whispering Woods is under the Rebellion's protection," Glimmer said. "You were lucky to make it as far as you did."

She turned to the boy. "Come on, Bow. Let's get this spy back to Bright Moon, where she can be interrogated properly."

Bright Moon! I can't let them take me there! Remembering her training, Adora assessed the situation and made a plan. First, she had to get out of her handcuffs. Then she'd have to find some way to escape her captors. The boy called Bow had a bow and arrows. She'd have to outrun them. Then there was that sparkly princess, Glimmer. How far could she teleport? What other powers did she have?

While Adora calculated this, they marched on through the woods.

"You're positive we're going the right way, Glimmer?" Bow asked.

"I know what I'm doing, Bow!" Glimmer snapped, but Adora could tell she was confused. She kept staring at a display pad and frowning. "Can you please just trust me for once?"

"You know I trust you," Bow replied. "But I'm starting to get a little freaked out. I mean, I pretty much grew up in these woods, and I've never seen this part of them. I've heard stories about weird stuff out here."

"It's fine, okay?" Glimmer insisted. "Just let me figure this out."

"Okay, okay," Bow said.

Frustrated, Glimmer teleported away. Bow turned to Adora with a friendly smile.

"Sorry about her," Bow said. "Usually she's really nice."

Yeah, right, Adora thought. *As if nice princesses exist.*

"Not much for talking, huh?" Bow asked.

"I prefer not to swap pleasantries with my captors," Adora replied coldly.

"Fair," Bow conceded. "Suit yourself."

They reached Glimmer, who had transported on top of a boulder. She peered into the distance and then consulted her display pad.

Adora glanced from the evil princess to the friendly boy next to her. He didn't seem like a vicious rebel.

Maybe he's lost, too, she thought.

"You know she's a princess, right?" Adora asked. "How can you follow her? Princesses are a dangerous threat to everyone in Etheria."

"Is that what Hordak told you?" Bow asked.

"Well, I thought it was just common knowl-edge," Adora replied, shrugging. "Princesses are violent instigators who don't even know how to control their powers."

As if on cue, Glimmer let out an angry scream and teleported yet again. *See?* Adora thought.

Bow smiled. "You've never actually met a prin-cess, have you?"

Adora shook her head. "Not in person, but—"

Glimmer gasped, and Adora and Bow hurried to catch up to her. She was frozen in place, staring at the remains of what Adora assumed had once been a village. It was scorched black.

"What happened to this place?" Adora asked.

"Don't play dumb with me!" Glimmer said. "I bet you were part of the raiding party that did this."

"What are you talking about?" Adora asked. "The Horde didn't do this!"

Glimmer grabbed Adora's arm and led her to a

broken-down robot. Painted on the side was the unmistakable logo of the Horde.

It . . . it can't be! Adora thought, her mind reeling. *The Horde doesn't destroy! We are fighting against the tyranny of evil princess rulers!*

"You're a heartless destroyer, just like all the rest of your people," Glimmer said. Tears glistened in the corners of her eyes.

"I am not a destroyer!" Adora protested. "Hordak says that we're doing what's best for Etheria. We're trying to make things better. More orderly."

"*This* is what's best for Etheria?" Glimmer asked, her voice choking as she gestured toward the burnt-out village. "Ever since the Horde got here, it's been poisoning our land, burning our cities, destroying everything in its path. And you're a part of it. How's that for orderly?"

She angrily marched away from Adora.

"This doesn't make any sense," Adora said. "The Horde would never do something like this."

"Did you really not know any of this?" Bow asked. "I mean, your army is called the *Evil* Horde."

"Who calls us that?" Adora asked.

"*Everybody!*" Bow replied.

This can't be true, Adora thought. *Maybe it's a trick.*

Her eyes returned to the Horde logo on the robot.

It doesn't make sense!

"The Horde rescued me when I was a baby and gave me a home," she told Bow. "They're my family. You don't know them like I do."

"Or maybe *you* don't know them like you think you do," Bow said.

Adora shuddered. *Could that be possible?* The idea was frightening.

A loud crashing sound from the woods up ahead interrupted her thoughts. Glimmer came tearing down the path.

"There's something out there!" she cried. "Something big!"

Bow pulled out his bow and arrows. "How big?"

Boom! The ground rocked beneath their feet, sending them all flying. Trees buckled and cracked as an enormous robot insect emerged from the ground, screeching.

Aaaaaaiiiiiiiieeeeeeeeeeeeee!

CHAPTER 12
FOR THE HONOR OF GRAYSKULL!

Adora's adrenaline raced as the insect turned its multiple bulbous eyes on them. One foot crashed down near Glimmer, but she teleported away. She reappeared up a tree at face level with the creature. Then she leapt onto its face, hitting it with a glittery zap.

Pretty bold move, Adora thought. She wanted to fight, too, but she still had on those stupid handcuffs. The insect turned to her, gnashing its pincers. Bow fired an arrow made of some kind of sticky substance, and the monster's jaws stuck shut. It fell forward, and Adora clumsily hopped out of the way, landing face-first in a bush.

I really need to get these handcuffs off! she thought as Glimmer blasted the creature with more sparkly attacks. It snapped its jaws, breaking free from the sticky substance. Then it clipped Glimmer with one of its pincers and sent her flying into a tree.

Bow fired a lasso arrow at the insect, pulling it back away from Glimmer as she slowly regained consciousness.

Adora picked herself up. She needed to find something to cut the handcuffs with.

Then she spotted the sword lying on the forest floor. She leaned down and managed to clumsily grasp the sword in her hands. She moved her cuffs back and forth against the sharp blade, trying to break them.

"Hey, bug brain!" she yelled.

The beast turned away from Bow and Glimmer.

"Come on, magic sword," Adora muttered. "Where's a blinding flash of light when you need one?"

The giant bug took flight and zoomed toward

Adora. Desperately, she raised the sword as best she could with her hands still bound.

Clang! The sword clashed with the metal talons of the monster. White light flashed, and the bug seemed to freeze. The sword's blade grew brighter and brighter.

Images flashed through Adora's mind. The planet Etheria, hanging in space. Strange ships flying through the sky. A city of towering buildings that Adora didn't recognize. A bright sky over the buildings, filled with planets.

Then she saw the majestic woman from her first vision, her face bursting with bright light. She lifted the sword about her head.

Light Hope's voice rang in Adora's head. *Will you fight for the honor of Grayskull?*

Somehow, Adora knew what she had to do. She raised the sword over her head, just like the woman in her vision.

"For the honor of Grayskull!" Adora cried.

The sword grew brighter and brighter. Adora floated up into the air, bathed in light. Her body spun, and her hair fell loose from its ponytail. The handcuffs broke apart.

As energy pulsed through her body, Adora felt stronger than she ever had before. She could conquer anything.

As if the robot heard her thoughts, it lowered its head and dropped to its knees, suddenly calm.

Moments later, the light faded and Adora landed back to the ground. Glimmer and Bow were staring at her, openmouthed. She examined herself and realized she was no longer wearing her Horde uniform, but a white body suit with a skirt and a golden emblem on the front. Gold wristbands. Gold-and-white boots. She felt something on her head and reached up to touch it—a crown with a jewel in front and wings on the sides. Her hair—no longer sensible and sandy-blonde, but long and full and shining like yellow gold—flowed out behind her along with a red cape.

Adora gasped. She had transformed into the warrior from her vision!

CHAPTER 13
THE FIRST ONES

"Ahhhhh!" Adora shrieked. She dropped the sword.

What is going on?!?!

She staggered back and fell to the ground. The energy and the strength from before left her. She was Adora again.

Pop! Glimmer teleported to the dropped sword in a shower of sparkles. Adora lunged and they both grabbed it at the same time.

"What did you do to me?" Adora asked.

"What do you mean, what did I do to you?" Glimmer shot back.

"I didn't know being a princess was contagious!" Adora yelled.

Bow ran in between them and put one hand on the sword.

"Okay, okay, everyone calm down," he said. He turned to Adora. "You wanna tell us how you did that?"

"I didn't do anything!" Adora protested. "All I did was pick up the sword, and then . . . whoosh! I'm in a tiara!"

"I don't care how she did it," Glimmer said. "We just have to make sure she NEVER DOES IT AGAIN!"

Glimmer gave the sword another tug. Then . . . *Aaaaiiiieeeeeee!*

No longer calm, the giant robot bug stomped toward them.

"We have to go!" Glimmer shouted.

They ran through the forest, chased by the bug. They crashed through the underbrush and finally stumbled down a slope that deposited them into a wide clearing. For now, at least, they had lost the monster.

Adora brushed leaves off her uniform and looked around. There were symbols carved into the forest floor, leading to the huge door of an ancient building.

"What is this place?" Adora asked. The symbols on the door looked strangely familiar.

Suddenly, the creature tore down the slope toward them.

"No idea!" Bow said. He pointed to the door. "But in there's got to be better than out here!"

They tried to open the door, but it wouldn't budge.

"Everyone grab on. I can get us in there!" Glimmer said.

"Glimmer, no!" Bow cried. "You've never teleported three people before!"

"Do you have a better idea?" Glimmer asked.

Adora did.

"This writing on the door looks like some kind of password," she said.

"You can read that?" Bow asked quickly. The robot was getting dangerously close.

Adora nodded. "You can't?"

"What's it say?" Bow asked.

Impossibly, the symbols' meaning popped into her head. "Eternia."

The ground beneath them rumbled. The door shuddered and then dissolved, revealing a dark passage behind it.

Adora sprinted inside, and Bow and Glimmer followed. The door appeared again, right in the giant bug's face.

Thud! The bug hit the outside of the door. Then there was silence.

All three of them collapsed to the ground, breathing hard. In the darkness, Adora's mind was reeling. Had she ever seen writing like that before? How could she read it?

Glimmer created a sparkle orb that added some dim light to the darkness.

Bow looked at Adora. "So, Horde soldier. Have you always been able to read First Ones writing?"

"Want to tell us exactly what's going on here?" Glimmer added.

Adora was just as confused as they were. "I told you, I don't know. I just read the word on the door."

"Right, you just read a word in a language that no one's spoken for a thousand years, and the door just opened into a mysterious ruin," Glimmer said with a sarcastic laugh. "Sure."

Adora jumped to her feet. "You think I did this on purpose? You think I wanted to be a princess? Princesses are monsters!"

Glimmer got up and into Adora's face. "Monsters? You're the monster!"

Bow pushed them apart. "Whoa, Glimmer, she did save us!"

"I don't care!" Glimmer shot back. "We can't trust her, Bow! Or have you forgotten everything the Horde's done to us? The people we've lost?"

She choked on the last word and turned away, and Adora realized she was holding back tears again.

Her emotions are real, Adora thought. *She's not lying. The Horde must have done some terrible things. But it's still so hard to believe . . .*

Glimmer turned to Bow.

"We need to find another way out of here and get her back to Bright Moon as soon as possible," she said. "My mother will know what to do with her."

Bow gave Adora an apologetic shrug as Glimmer marched ahead of them.

Adora knew she could break away from Bow and run away. *But where would I go?* she wondered. *If I go back outside, I'll be fighting that creature by myself, with no weapon. I need to get that sword back.*

"Hey, so, thanks for saving us from that bug thing back there when you could have escaped instead," Bow said.

"Okay, well, I didn't save you," Adora replied. "I just wanted to get the sword, okay?"

"Are you sure it's not because you secretly like us?" Bow asked.

"Wh—I don't like you!" Adora protested. "You're my captors!"

"Sure," Bow said, with a grin. "Thanks for saving us, anyway. I'm Bow, by the way."

Adora started to smile back but stopped herself. "Adora," she said gruffly.

They caught up to Glimmer. She was holding up the sword and muttering to herself, standing in front of a stone with more carvings on it.

She's trying to see if it will work for her, Adora realized. *But somehow . . . I can feel it . . . the sword will only respond to me.*

"Look at those carvings," Glimmer said when Adora and Bow approached. "I think this might be a First Ones ruin."

"What's a First One?" Adora finally asked.

Glimmer raised her eyebrows. "You've never heard of the First Ones?"

Adora shrugged.

"The First Ones are the original settlers of Etheria," Bow explained. "They disappeared a thousand years ago, but they left behind a lot of old ruins and technology. Like this place."

"So what happened to them?" Adora asked.

"No one knows," Bow replied. "They just . . . disappeared. The Horde didn't tell you about them?"

Adora frowned. "Seems like there's a lot the Horde didn't tell me."

"So how do we get out of here?" Glimmer asked impatiently.

Bow gazed around at the maze of dark hallways around them. "Wanna turn on some lights, Adora?"

"I don't know how to do that," she replied.

"Maybe there's a magic word!" Bow suggested. "What is the First Ones' word for 'lights'?"

Adora threw up her hands. Who did these people think she was? "I don't know! I'm not magic!"

"Obviously," Glimmer said. "Everyone stand back."

Glimmer began to form a sparkly orb between her palms.

"Uh, Glimmer, maybe you should take it easy?" Bow said. "We're a long way from Bright Moon. It'll be a while until you can recharge."

"Bow!" Glimmer said, scowling.

"You have to recharge your powers?" Adora asked. Glimmer couldn't be that powerful or dangerous if that was the case.

"Can we NOT talk about this in front of the Horde soldier?" Glimmer snapped at Bow. "Now, stand back!"

Glimmer took a deep breath. She made a straining sound as she used all of her effort to light up the chamber.

Immediately, Adora's eye was drawn to a huge figure in the middle of the room—a statue of the warrior woman with flowing hair, holding a sword just like one she had found.

"Oh, hey! That's you!" Bow said, pointing to the statue.

"What?" Adora asked. "That doesn't look anything like me."

"No, I mean the other you," Bow said. "The scary one in the cape."

Adora reached out and touched the inscription on the base of the statue. "That was . . . me?"

"You can read that inscription, right?" Bow asked. "What does it say?"

Adora looked at the inscription. "It says . . . She-Ra."

As she spoke, the inscription blazed with light.

CHAPTER 14
ADORA'S CHOICE

The light spread from the inscription through the base of the statue, then spread out across the floor of the chamber and up the walls. A ghostly image of a woman in a long gown began to appear in front of them. It flickered weakly.

"What is that thing?" Adora whispered.

"Greetings, administrator," the figure said in a robotic voice. "What is your query?"

Bow and Glimmer ducked behind Adora.

"I think it's some kind of ancient hologram," Bow guessed in a whisper.

"What is your query?" the hologram repeated.

Bow spoke up. "Uh, hi. What is this place?"

The hologram didn't respond. Adora considered

speaking up, but her thoughts were still reeling with everything she had learned. *Princesses might not be evil. First Ones disappeared a thousand years ago. Somehow I turn into a princess named She-Ra?*

Bow tried talking to the hologram again. "How do we get out of here?"

The hologram flickered. "What is your query?"

Bow sighed.

The hologram flickered again. "Administrator not detected," it said.

Uh-oh, Adora thought. *This can't be good . . .*

The bright lights filling the chamber suddenly changed, becoming an eerie purple.

Creeeeeeeeak!

The sound came from somewhere deep in the ground. The whole room began to shake.

"Lockdown initiated," the hologram said.

"No! No lockdown!" Bow yelled.

The room around them began to change. The panels of the walls shifted and slid. The ground beneath their feet began to lower.

Panicked, Adora glanced at the door they had come through. Now a panel of the wall covered it. There was no way out!

"Adora, you gotta get it to stop!" Bow cried.

"What makes you think I can?!" Adora asked.

"Query not recognized," the hologram repeated.

"There's got to be a password or something!" Bow said as the walls around them continued to move, groaning loudly. "You can read their writing!"

A sudden jolt of the floor tested their balance. A spray of sparks flew from one of the wall panels, along with a sickening groan of gears.

"Stop it!" Adora yelled. "Uh . . . Eternia! Eternia!"

But the password she used before didn't work. Desperate, she turned to Glimmer.

"Give me the sword!" she demanded.

"What? No!" Glimmer held the sword closer to her.

"We need the scary lady in the cape!" Adora said. "I don't know how, but she's the key to this place. So maybe she can get us out!"

"You're a Horde soldier! I'm not giving you the sword!" Glimmer said.

Crash! A wall panel fell just feet away from them. The hologram flickered and disappeared. Adora shouted out every possible password she could think of.

"Uh, Eternia! Cape! She-Ra!"

A grinding sound came from above, and a portion of the ceiling groaned and started to plummet toward them. The three of them huddled in fear, bracing for the impact.

"Hold on!" Glimmer yelled.

"Glimmer, no!" Bow cried.

Glimmer, Bow, and Adora exploded in sparkling pink light and vanished just as a chunk of the ceiling fell. They appeared outside—high above the Whispering Woods!

Adora and Bow screamed as they plummeted to the ground.

"Glimmer!" Bow yelled.

Adora glanced over and saw that Glimmer's eyes were closed. As they fell, Bow took an arrow from his quiver and shot it straight down. The arrow unfurled into a gossamer net that lashed onto the trees, forming a makeshift safety net.

Whomp! They crashed through the branches and landed in the net.

Adora bounced a few times. When the net had settled, she crawled over to Bow. He was kneeling over the princess, a look of concern on his face.

Adora nodded. Together, they carried Glimmer out of the net and rested her body on the forest floor. They waited, anxiously, for a long time.

I hope she's okay, Adora thought, and then a moment later, *What's happening to me? I'm worried about a princess?!*

At one point, Bow went off to find some water and Adora realized she was alone with the sleeping princess. This was her chance—she could run, go back to the Horde, and report everything she'd seen and learned. But she had so many questions . . .

Finally, Glimmer's eyes fluttered open.

"Glimmer!" Bow cried.

"Did the teleporting work?" Glimmer asked, her voice weak.

"Yeah, it worked. Barely. Are you all right?" Bow asked.

"I'm fine," Glimmer replied. She tried to sit up, but then she winced in pain. "Ugh. I think I used too much power getting us out of there."

"I don't know who could've predicted that," Bow teased. "Me. Like, an hour ago."

Adora smiled to herself. Their teasing reminded her of her friendship with Catra.

But Glimmer wasn't amused. "Bow!"

"Sorry! I'm just glad you're okay," he said. "No more teleporting for a while, okay? You could really hurt yourself."

"I'm fine, okay?" Glimmer said. "Let's just get back to Bright Moon so I can recharge already."

Then she noticed Adora. "Why are you still here? You could've escaped at any time."

Adora hesitated. She didn't owe this princess an answer. It wasn't like she was chatting with Catra, sharing her feelings with a friend. And yet, something told Adora that Glimmer was actually interested. That she cared.

"I just . . . I want to figure out what's happening to me," Adora said. "And if I go back to the Fright Zone, I'll never know."

She looked away from them. "I never knew where I came from—who my family was. Shadow Weaver says it doesn't matter who I was before—that I was nothing before Hordak took me in. There's always been a part of me that I just don't know anything about. And all of this—it feels familiar, somehow. I don't know how else to explain it." Adora stopped. Had she ever shared something that important with someone other than Catra? It felt weird, but also maybe . . . good?

Bow's face lit up. "Glimmer's mom knows more about First Ones tech than anyone," he said. "She'll know what's going on with you and the sword for sure. So if you want your questions answered, stick with us."

He looked to Glimmer for approval. She took the sword and used it to prop herself up.

"Let's go," she said. "There should be a village a few miles from here. They'll be able to give us a ride back to Bright Moon."

Glimmer slowly limped down the path. Bow smiled hopefully at Adora.

Adora looked behind her. She could go back to the Horde. Become a force captain, like she'd always wanted. Convince Shadow Weaver to let Catra be on her team.

She looked ahead at Glimmer. Or, she could go with a princess, the enemy of the Horde, and try to find out what the sword meant. Who this She-Ra was. And her place in it all.

It would be an easy decision if it weren't for one thing, or rather, one person: Catra. How could Adora leave her behind? But a few days ago, when Adora had shared with Catra that she wanted to find out more about Etheria and herself, Catra had understood, right?

From down the path, the sword glinted in Glimmer's hand, and Adora felt a pull from it.

She jogged up to Bow and Glimmer.

"I'm coming with you," she said.

ABOUT THE AUTHOR

Tracey West has written more than 300 books for children and young adults, including the following series: Pixie Tricks, Hiro's Quest, and Dragon Masters. She has appeared on the *New York Times* bestseller list as author of the Pokémon chapter book adaptations. Tracey currently lives with her family in New York State's Catskill Mountains. She can be found on Twitter at @TraceyWestBooks.